Robby
Visits the Doctor

written by
Martine Davison

illustrated by
Nancy Stevenson

Random House 🏠 New York

Library of Congress Cataloging-in-Publication Data

Davison, Martine. Robby visits the doctor / by Martine Davison ; illustrated by Nancy Stevenson. p. cm. — (An AMA kids book) Summary: Robby wakes up with a bad earache, but he feels better after going to the doctor and taking several doses of medicine. ISBN 0-679-81819-7 (trade) — ISBN 0-679-91819-1 (lib. bdg.) [1. Earache—Fiction. 2. Medical care—Fiction.] I. Stevenson, Nancy, ill. II. Title. III. Series. PZ7.D3215Ro 1992 [E]—dc20 91-30193 Manufactured in the United States of America 10 9 8 7 6 5 4 3 2 1

One Saturday morning Robby woke up feeling
sick and crabby. He was hot and sweaty. And he
had an awful, terrible, dreadful earache.
    "Mommy! Daddy!" he called downstairs.
"I don't feel good!"

His mother and father came into his bedroom. "What's the trouble, sport?" his father asked.

"My ear hurts!" Robby moaned.

Robby's mother sat down on the edge of the bed. She felt Robby's forehead.

"Hmmmm. You do feel warm. Maybe that cold you had last week went into your ear. I'll call and find out if the doctor can see you today."

Robby felt scared. He didn't want to go to the doctor's office. Checkups were one thing. Being sick was another!

In a few minutes, his mother returned, smiling. "Good news, Robby. The doctor's office said that if you're sick, they'll make time to see you."

Robby's father helped him get dressed.

After Robby brushed his teeth

and washed his face,

came downstairs to the kitchen.
mother gave him a glass of
favorite juice, Very Very Berry.

In the car Robby got to sit up front. His father slipped a small pillow behind Robby's head.

"What's the doctor going to do?" Robby wondered nervously.

"Look in your ear and find out why it's hurting you. Then she'll probably give you some medicine to take to make you feel better. Don't worry."

But Robby did worry.

"Hi, Robby!" said Glenda, the receptionist in the office of Hillsdale Pediatric Associates. "Come on in and have a seat in the sick room. Dr. Robinson will see you soon."

Robby had never even noticed before that there were two waiting rooms here: one for sick children and one for well ones.

Now he was more nervous than ever! "I've never had to wait in the sick room before."

The room was very crowded. Robby took a seat. He reached for his father's hand and looked around.

There was a girl sniffling with a cold and a boy lying down, resting his head on his mother's lap.

Babies were crying. The phone was ringing. This sure was a busy place!

"Want to check out those toys?" Robby's father asked him, pointing to a shelf full of toys in the corner.

"I don't feel like it," Robby said. "My ear hurts too much."

Just then Dr. Robinson came out of one of the examining rooms. A boy was with her.

It was Kevin, Robby's friend!

Robby waved and Kevin came over.

"Hi, Rob. I stepped on a rusty nail. I had to get the sore cleaned and get a shot. What are you here for?"

"I've got this killer earache," Robby said.

"Don't be scared. They'll fix you up," Kevin said.

Robby waved good-bye to his friend. Then he said to his father, "Will I have to get a shot too?"

"I doubt it," his father said, but he didn't seem all that sure.

Now Robby had something new to worry about.

"What do you say we read a book?" Robby's father suggested. He went over to the shelves and came back with a book on Robby's favorite subject: dinosaurs!

"Did baby pterodactyls ever get earaches?" Robby wondered. He couldn't tell from the pictures whether they even had ears.

Just then Nurse Jackie came in.
"Hi, Robby," she said. "Go on into the room with the red door.
I'll be right with you."

Robby and his father went into the examining room with the red door.

Nurse Jackie came in and laid out some clean instruments and a folder with Robby's name on it.

"Robby, please take off your shirt and sweater. You can leave your pants and shoes on."

Robby's father helped him off with his clothes. Then he boosted Robby up on the examining table. It was covered with clean white paper that crackled when Robby sat on it.

"Are you cold, Robby?" asked Nurse Jackie. "You can put this sheet around your shoulders."

Nurse Jackie asked Robby and his father about when he got the cold and when his ear started hurting. She wrote everything down.

"I'm going to take your temperature, Robby," Nurse Jackie said. "Open your mouth, please." She placed a thermometer under Robby's tongue. After about a minute the thermometer beeped.

Nurse Jackie showed Robby he red digital numbers on the ermometer. They said 101.6°.

"A normal temperature is 8.6°," Jackie explained. "Your mperature is higher than that day." She wrote that down, too.

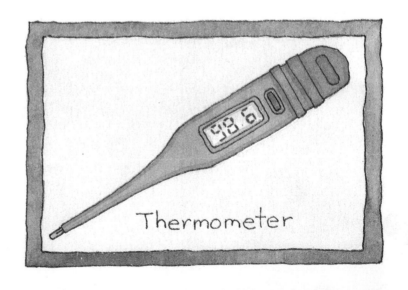

Thermometer

Dr. Robinson came in the very next moment.

"Okay, Robby! Let's see what the problem is." Dr. Robinson gently felt Robby's neck and looked in his eyes and his nose. "Now open your mouth really wide and say 'ahhh' for me."

The doctor held down Robby's tongue with a tongue depressor and looked down his throat with a small flashlight.

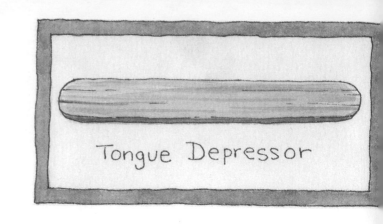

Tongue Depressor

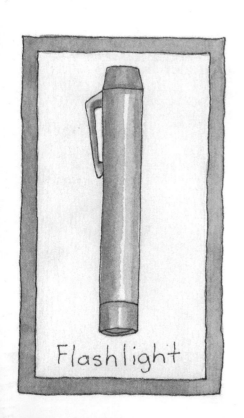

Flashlight

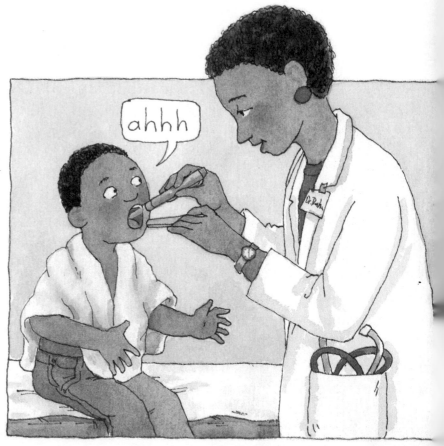

ahhh

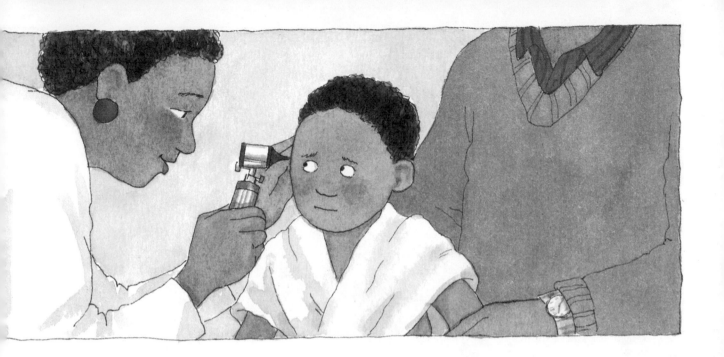

"Now I'm going to look into your ear and see what's causing the pain. This is called an otoscope." She showed Robby the instrument. "It helps me see way inside your ears."

Robby whimpered. His dad took his hand and squeezed it. Dr. Robinson looked in one ear and then the other.

"I can see why you feel bad! Your left eardrum is red. The germs from your cold have caused an infection in your ear," the doctor explained.

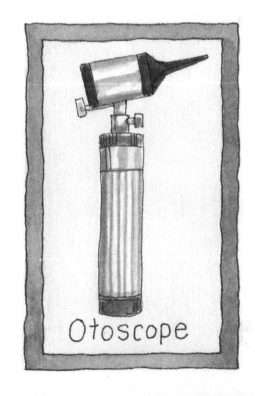

Otoscope

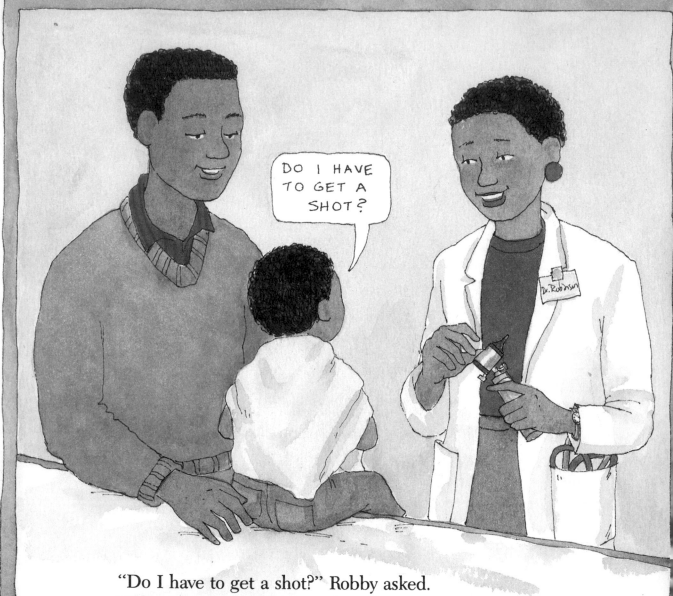

"Do I have to get a shot?" Robby asked.

"Oh, no!" Dr. Robinson said. "I'll just give you some medicine to make the infection go away."

"Would you like to see my eardrum, Robby?" asked Dr. Robinson, holding out the otoscope with a clean tip.

"Gee, could I?" said Robby, brightening up. His father helped him put the tip of the instrument in Dr. Robinson's ear.

"See that round white thing? That's my eardrum," Dr. Robinson said. "When I look in your ear, your eardrum is pink because of the infection."

Robby couldn't wait to tell Kevin that he had seen the doctor's eardrum.

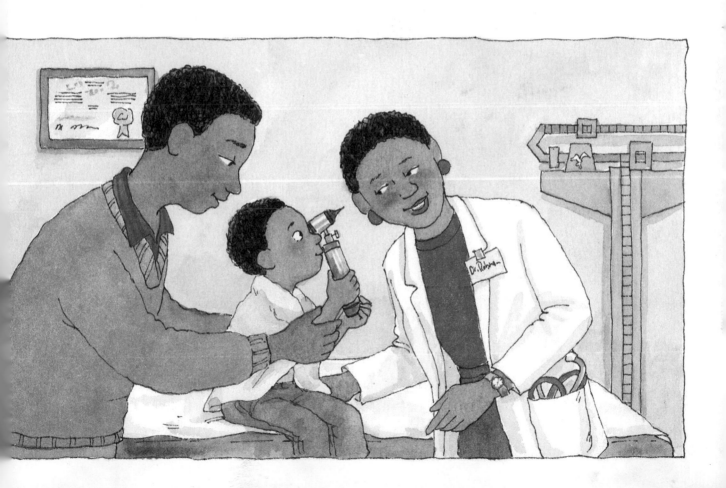

"You can get dressed now, Robby," Dr. Robinson told him.
While Robby put his shirt on, the doctor spoke to Robby's father.

"He's got an ear infection—but it's nothing to worry about. I'll
write you a prescription for an antibiotic. He should take it three
times a day for the next ten days." The doctor smiled at Robby.
"Even when you start to feel better, you should still take the
medicine. Then you'll be good as new."

"If you feel better on Monday, you can go back to school, Robby. But remember, you have to keep on taking the medicine. That way the infection will heal and your ear will feel all better. And for a few days, wear a hat when you play outside."

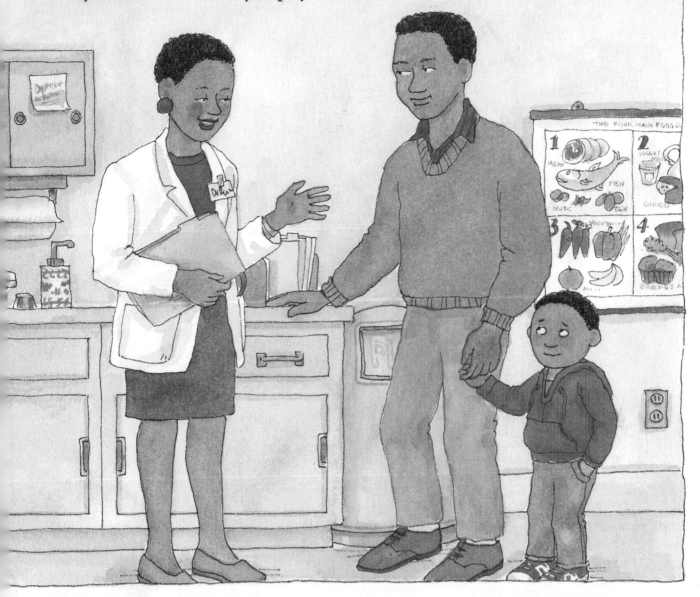

At the reception desk Nurse Jackie gave Robby's father the prescription. Robby got to choose a sticker. He chose one of a pterodactyl. Jackie told Robby's dad, "Call us on Monday if his temperature is still above 99° or his ear still hurts."

On the way home they stopped at the pharmacy to get the prescription filled.

Robby sat in a chair and held his head. "I went to the doctor and I still feel bad."

"That's because you have an infection. We'll get this medicine and go right home," his dad told him. "Hang in there, sport."

At home Robby got to lie in his parents' big bed and watch TV. His mother sat on the bed and held out a spoonful of medicine.

"Yuck," said Robby, and covered his mouth with both hands.

"It's cherry-flavored," his mother coaxed, "and you know how you love cherries."

Robby dropped his hands. He swallowed the medicine and made a face. "But my ear still hurts!" he complained.

"That's why I'm giving you this other medicine, too. To help ease the pain. As soon as you've taken a few more doses of the doctor's medicine, your ear will begin to stop hurting, I promise. Now, how about some chicken noodle soup and oyster crackers?"

On Monday Robby felt well enough to go back to school.

He had to go down to the nurse at lunchtime to take his medicine. But his ear hardly hurt at all anymore. He even played dodgeball in gym.

By Wednesday he felt good as new.

Kevin came over after school. They decided to play outside.

"Just a second!" said Robby. "Dr. Robinson said I need to wear a hat for a few days so my earache doesn't come back. No way am I getting another earache if I can help it!"

Robby put on his hat and ran outside to play with Kevin.